The Mighty Midwest Flood

Titles in the *American Disasters* series:

The Exxon Valdez
Tragic Oil Spill
ISBN 0-7660-1058-9

Fire in Oakland, California
Billion-Dollar Blaze
ISBN 0-7660-1220-4

Hurricane Andrew
Nature's Rage
ISBN 0-7660-1057-0

The L.A. Riots
Rage in the City of Angels
ISBN 0-7660-1219-0

The Mighty Midwest Flood
Raging Rivers
ISBN 0-7660-1221-2

The Oklahoma City Bombing
Terror in the Heartland
ISBN 0-7660-1061-9

Plains Outbreak Tornadoes
Killer Twisters
ISBN 0-7660-1059-7

San Francisco Earthquake, 1989
Death and Destruction
ISBN 0-7660-1060-0

The Siege at Waco
Deadly Inferno
ISBN 0-7660-1218-2

TWA Flight 800
Explosion in Midair
ISBN 0-7660-1217-4

The World Trade Center Bombing
Terror in the Towers
ISBN 0-7660-1056-2

The Mighty Midwest Flood

Raging Rivers

Carmen Bredeson

Enslow Publishers, Inc.

40 Industrial Road   PO Box 38
Box 398   Aldershot
Berkeley Heights, NJ   07922   Hants GU12 6BP
USA   UK

http://www.enslow.com

Library of Congress Cataloging-in-Publication Data

Bredeson, Carmen.
    The mighty midwest flood : raging rivers / Carmen Bredeson.
      p. cm. — (American disasters)
    Includes bibliographical references and index.
    Summary: Details the disastrous floods that occurred in nine
midwestern states when ten times the average amount of rain fell
during the spring and early summer of 1993.
    ISBN 0-7660-1221-2
    1. Floods—Middle West—Juvenile literature. [1. Floods—Middle
West.] I. Title. II. Series.
GB1399.4.M6B74 1999
363.34'93'0978—dc21   98-11728
                                              CIP
                                              AC

Printed in the United States of America

10 9 8 7 6 5 4 3 2 1

To Our Readers:
All Internet addresses in this book were active and appropriate when we went to press.
Any comments or suggestions can be sent by e-mail to Comments@enslow.com or to
the address on the back cover.

Illustration Credits: AP/Wide World Photos, pp. 1, 6, 8, 10, 11, 12, 14, 16, 17,
18, 21, 22, 23, 24, 25, 28, 30, 35, 38, 40, 41.

Cover Illustration: AP/Wide World Photos.

Contents

As families scrambled to escape the rising floodwaters, many pets were left behind. This marooned cat, soaked with oil and water, waits for a rescuer.

CHAPTER 1

Triumph and Tragedy

As the sun rose on a sticky August morning in 1993, Glen Grotegeers heard the welcome whirr of a helicopter. The Illinois farmer had just spent a sleepless night in a tree, marooned by muddy brown floodwater. All through the night he had wondered whether he would ever see his four children again. Now, Grotegeers grabbed his orange life jacket and began to wave it frantically in the air. "I thought it was going to be like Rescue 911," he said. "The helicopter's going to come and they're going to drop a line down to me, and everything was going to be swell."[1]

The day before, Grotegeers had been out in a small boat, drifting around the swamp that used to be his farm. Suddenly a floating tree trunk rammed the boat, and he was thrown into the stinking water. Gasping and sputtering, he surfaced and looked around. The boat was being carried away by the strong current. Grotegeers felt himself being swept away in the same strong current, so he swam for the nearest tree. With no help in sight, the stranded farmer could do nothing but settle into the tree's branches for a long, uncomfortable night.

In the morning, as the rumbling rescue helicopter approached, Grotegeers thought his ordeal was finally over. However, instead of stopping for the frantically signaling man, the copter flew away. Apparently the crew was looking in another direction and did not see Grotegeers. After waiting for several more hours, Grotegeers finally decided that he would have to save himself. He jumped into the water, then swam and floated for twenty miles

*P*eg and Ben Northstine pull a small boat through a flooded cornfield. Glen Grotegeers was thrown from a similar boat when a tree trunk rammed into it.

before reaching a levee, or retaining wall, where he could climb ashore.

Twenty-one hours after his ordeal had begun, Grotegeers was finally safe. Gena Giggins, a ranger with the United States Army Corps of Engineers, was amazed that the farmer had managed to survive the trip in the Mississippi River. She said, "There [was] so much debris coming down the river, something could have hit him in the head."[2] The swollen river was full of tree trunks, pieces of houses, snakes, and animal carcasses.

In addition to many people, thousands of animals, both wild and domestic, were victims of these floods. Animals that had managed not to drown were perched in trees, on rooftops, and on any dry spot they could find. As rescue teams patrolled the floodwaters in boats, they were able to save many stranded animals. Disaster services coordinator Terri Crisp said, "The animals were so frightened that many of them jumped right into our arms. When we got them into the boat, we could actually hear them sigh in relief."[3]

In Randolph County, Illinois, Sheriff Ben Picou and his crew spent days rescuing hundreds of animals from the floodwaters. Sheriff Picou said that in one spot "there were twenty to twenty-five hogs hanging on [floating] bales of hay, hanging on [tree] limbs, even buckets."[4] His brother, David Picou, added, "I saw some on a tin roof with a skunk; they would get sunburned, then cool off in the water, then climb back on the roof."[5] The sheriff estimated that during this period they saved more than a

*A*n animal handler (left) and veterinarian Joel Pounds
(center) strain to rescue a horse from floodwaters near
Portage Des Sioux, Missouri.

thousand hogs and a hundred cats and dogs, along with
many rabbits, chickens, and coyotes.

Thousands more animals were not rescued and died
in the flood. Some, like the coyotes, were wild animals
that were swept out of the woods and into the swiftly
moving currents. Others were pets that became trapped in
houses and yards when the waters suddenly rose.
Sixteen-year-old Charles Loterebour lost his two-month-
old puppy, Tippy, when a levee broke in Des Moines,
Iowa. Charles said, "I fed him and then went down to
work on the dikes. When I got back, it [the water] was
already four feet deep in the backyard. His doghouse was
underwater and he was gone."[6]

Life and death dramas were being played out all over the American Midwest during the summer of 1993. Unusually heavy rainfall had sent streams and rivers spilling over their banks. Water covered farmlands and towns in nine states. Thousands of people were forced to evacuate as the floodwaters gradually filled their homes and businesses with muddy water. In addition to the loss of property, fifty-one people lost their lives during the devastating floods.

On July 23, 1993, a group of sixteen boys and four counselors set out on a hike in Cliff Cave Park, located in

A group of pigs finds higher ground atop a barn roof in Monroe County, Illinois.

*J*ennifer Metherd, age twenty-one, was one of the two counselors who drowned when a flash flood filled a cave in Cliff Cave Park.

South St. Louis County, Illinois. As the group walked through the soggy park, five of the boys and two of the counselors decided to explore one of the many caves that border the park's landscape. Water was already lapping up to their ankles as the explorers entered the dark cave.

Then all of a sudden, some of the kids hollered out that the water was rising.[7] A flash flood, caused by days of heavy rain, sent a sudden torrent of water cascading through sinkholes and into the cave. The boys and their counselors were knocked off their feet and swept deeper into the cave. Screams and cries filled the air as the hikers struggled to breathe.

Thirteen-year-old hiker Gary Mahr held his breath while the water gushed over him. When his head broke the water's surface, he grabbed a rock ledge and held on. Eighteen hours later, rescue workers found Gary, still clinging to the ledge, one thousand feet inside the cave. He had been there alone in the dark, all night. After the rescue, Gary told his mother, Sharon McRoberts, about the ordeal. Later, McRoberts said that her son "just tried to hold his breath as long as he could until he was able to float back up. Once he floated back up, he started reaching for something he could grab."[8]

Other members of the group were not so fortunate. The four boys and two counselors who had entered the cave with Gary all drowned when the flash flood washed them away.

While Gary was clinging to the ledge, his friends' bodies drifted past him. "He saw every last one that floated past. They bumped over him," said his mother.[9]

The Bayview (left) and Quincy Memorial bridges lead from
Quincy, Illinois (top), to West Quincy, Missouri (bottom),
here mostly underwater.

CHAPTER 2

Weather Patterns

During the spring of 1993, rain began to fall, slowly at first, and then harder and harder. After a time, the saturated ground could not absorb any more water. Rain collected in overflowing puddles and ditches. What had been lazy, meandering streams now started to look like raging rivers. As the water flowed, it met other streams and merged with them into powerful waterways. And still it rained.

A high-pressure weather system had parked itself along the eastern United States and was sucking warm moisture up from the Gulf of Mexico. At the same time, a band of northern air currents had moved south and brought cool air from Canada into the upper Midwest. As the cool air collided with warm moist air, thunderstorms erupted. Weeks passed, and the storms just stayed where they were, dumping more and more rain on the already saturated Midwest.

Army Corps of Engineers personnel estimated that ten

times the normal amount of rain fell on the Midwest during the spring and early summer of 1993. Corps engineer Bob Anderson said, "The outlook is bleak. The weather patterns are merciless."[1] Armstrong, Iowa, received ten inches of rain in four hours on June 23. Adrian, Minnesota, received seven inches of rain in a little over an hour on July 10.[2] The story was much the same in parts of Wisconsin, North Dakota, South Dakota, Nebraska, Kansas, Illinois, and Missouri.

There was only one place for all the water to end up—in the Mississippi River. Throughout the upper Midwest, small streams empty into larger streams, then into rivers,

Weeks of heavy rain in the Midwest flooded many farms, like the one pictured here, ruining crops and causing major property damage.

*T*his infrared image, taken by a NASA ER-2 aircraft, shows the Mississippi and Missouri rivers flowing into each other. Vegetation can be seen in red; urban areas are in blue or white. Homes and other buildings caught in the floods appear as white dots in the water.

and eventually into the great Mississippi. The thousands of waterways that feed the Mississippi are called its tributaries. Called the Father of Waters by American Indians, the Mississippi River and its tributaries drain one third of the United States. Flooding on any of the tributaries means that the Mississippi will receive more water than normal. Flooding on many of the tributaries at one time can spell disaster for the people who live along the banks of the mighty river.

The source of the Mississippi River is Lake Itasca, located in Minnesota. From there, the Mississippi flows through the heartland of the United States and empties into the Gulf of Mexico, 2,340 miles later. Along the river lies some of the richest farmland in the country. Periodic flooding has left deposits of silt on the land that enrich the soil. Because of the rich land, people throughout the ages have settled along the Mississippi to live and grow crops. Small towns and large cities grew up around the farmers' settlements and dot the river's banks.

*B*arges remained idle not only on the Mississippi River, but also on its tributaries. Here, idle barges along the Illinois River stack up in Spring Valley, Illinois.

In order to protect their towns and land, many communities built levees to hold back the water that rises during flood times. The levees are huge walls that are made of dirt, sand, and sometimes concrete. They keep rising rivers from spilling over and reaching the towns and farmlands. Before levees were built, the water gradually overflowed its banks and spread out onto the land.

As more runoff from small streams and tributaries collects in the Mississippi River, its water level rises and the current flows faster. During the flood of 1993, the Mississippi River current became so dangerous that all boat and barge traffic had to be halted for two months. Fifteen percent of all freight in the United States is carried by Mississippi barges. Normally, there are thousands of these barges traveling up and down the river, carrying such cargo as machinery, coal, grain, and fertilizer. In the summer of 1993, when the river was closed to traffic, more than five thousand barges were left sitting idle.

In addition to halting barge traffic on a 585-mile stretch of the river, the high water submerged hundreds of miles of railroad tracks and closed many highways. On July 16, 1993, the Bayview Bridge between West Quincy, Missouri, and Quincy, Illinois, was closed. It had been the last bridge to remain open across the Mississippi River for two hundred miles. Now families that lived on opposite sides could no longer visit each other. People who lived on one side of the river and worked on the other could not get to their jobs. Not much was moving in the Midwest during the summer of 1993—except the raging water.

CHAPTER 3

Relentless Water

In July, in Des Moines, Iowa, a thunderstorm dumped four inches of rain in just four hours on the already saturated countryside. The normally small Raccoon River grew into a huge waterway. Pressure from the water built up on the town's levees. One finally gave way on July 10, sending floodwaters rolling through Des Moines. Tons of water were forced into the city's storm sewers with such pressure that manhole covers were blown into the air.

Water, mud, tree branches, and snakes gushed through doors and windows. People grabbed what belongings they could and ran for higher ground. Left behind were businesses and homes submerged in slime. One of the places hit hardest by the flood was the city's water treatment plant, which supplied drinking water to the two hundred fifty thousand residents of Des Moines. Its pumps and generators were under nine feet of water within minutes.

Suddenly the people in Des Moines had no drinking or

A man makes his way past flooded mailboxes in downtown West Des Moines, Iowa. High water from the nearby Raccoon River caused the evacuation of thirty-five hundred people there.

bathing water flowing into their homes. Mary Challender said, "It wasn't until we turned on the shower and were greeted with a sputtering of trapped air, or used the toilet and realized it wouldn't flush, that we began to gain an understanding of what we were in for."[1] On the average, every American uses fifty gallons of water a day for drinking, washing, and cooking. People can survive without baths or clean clothes, but they must have drinking water.

National Guard troops began arriving with tankers full

*T*he Peterson Paper Company in Davenport, Iowa, managed to stay open, despite being surrounded by water. Here, Don Estes rows back to the company dock after making a delivery.

of clean drinking water. People carrying empty containers formed long lines at the trucks, waiting patiently in the hot sun for their two gallons each of clean water. One man in Ohio loaded up his truck with bottled water and drove it all the way to Des Moines, just to help out however he could.

Although there was adequate water for drinking, there was none available for bathing during the two weeks that it took to repair the water treatment plant. For several days after the levee broke, rain stopped falling and the sun shone down brightly on the hot, dirty people in Des Moines. Three days after the flood, rain began falling again. People put on swimsuits, grabbed their soap and shampoo, and ran outside for a shower. It was a welcome event for those who had been trying to clean out the approximately twenty-one hundred homes and three hundred fifty businesses that had been swamped by the flood.

Everything in the flood's path was covered with gray mud that smelled of rotting plants and sewage. Pesticides, toxic runoff from factories, and dead animals all contributed to the horrible stench that filled the air.

*R*esidents of Alton, Illinois, wait patiently in line to fill jugs with clean drinking water.

*M*any people who were displaced by the floods had to find creative ways to shower or shave.

Even though the smell was awful, one woman said, "You know what the worst thing is? Worms. Big, long, wriggly night crawlers. They're everywhere. You pull back a bedspread and find worms in your bed, and, believe me, that's real discouraging."[2]

Some residents of Des Moines were living in shelters because their homes were flooded. They lost many of their belongings when the waters swept through town. Nine-year-old Kelly Dyer, whose bedroom wall and ceiling collapsed under the weight of the water, said, "The shelter is pretty fun. It's like a whole big family for everybody. The hardest part is knowing that you don't have a home to live in once we have to leave."[3]

As the residents of Des Moines struggled to put their lives back in order, assistance arrived from unexpected places. Neighbors who had not spoken to each other in years helped drag rotten carpeting from each other's

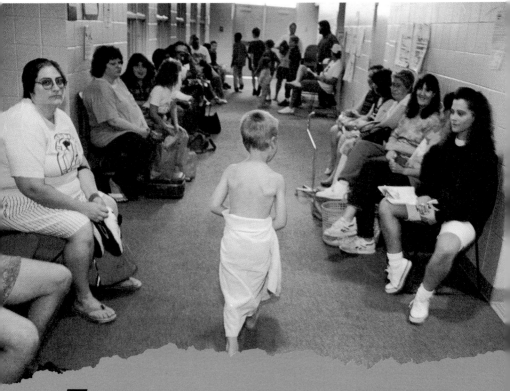

*F*ive-year-old Zack Reese of Des Moines showers at the local YMCA. Many flood victims made the best of their misfortune, enjoying the support of their communities.

homes. Young residents stood in the lines to obtain water for older members of the community. One woman said, "Awful as it's been, it's also been oddly wonderful. It's made the city into one big family."[4]

In Festus, Missouri, another community gathered together to offer their help during trying times. Kim Flieg and Scott Peters had their wedding scheduled for July 10. However, six feet of water surrounded the church where the ceremony was to take place. The church basement was flooded, and the water lapped at the steps leading into the sanctuary. Would the couple have to cancel the wedding that they had planned for so long?

Friends and relatives said definitely not and pitched in to build a barricade of sandbags so that no more water could get into the church. Peters' sixty-seven-year-old grandfather worked for twenty-three hours, pumping water out of the church basement. All the effort paid off, and the bride and groom were married with dry feet. Minister Richard Adams said, "It's important to us to be able to do a wedding like this. It shows people that every-thing is not out of control."[5]

After the wedding ceremony was over, the newlyweds turned and walked down the aisle. When they opened the doors of the church, they were greeted by the smiling faces of the sandbagging crew, along with a little surprise. Instead of the usual limousine to carry the couple away, there was a decorated aluminum canoe tied to the church railing. Charles Peters, the father of the groom, said,

"Everyone was surprised—especially the bride. Her mouth dropped wide open."[6]

People in East Hardin, Illinois, were facing a problem of their own. Rising water in the Mississippi River was backing up into the Illinois River and threatening the farmlands of East Hardin. Water was lapping at the top of the twenty-one-foot-tall Nutwood Levee. Everyone in town was filling sandbags, trying to build the levee higher. Men and women worked side by side with students, National Guard soldiers, and even inmates from the area prisons. Captain Pat Smallwood said, "I did more physical work yesterday than I've done since I did a twenty-six-mile road march in the Marine Corps. These people are really kicking butt. [There's] no whining, no complaining."[7]

On a farm outside East Hardin, the Lorton family was busy preparing their house and farm for the worst. Jeff and Sandy Lorton and their four teenage children had plenty to do. Three thousand hogs had to be moved to higher ground, along with their food. In the house, furniture was carried to the second floor to keep it from getting wet if the levee broke. Danielle and her brothers, J. D., Nate, and Laef, dumped clothes and personal belongings into the bed of a pickup truck. When the family members had done all that they could, they left their home to stay with relatives.

Despite the work of the sandbaggers, the Nutwood Levee was just not high enough to hold back the flood. Water began to spill over the top of the levee, slowly at first, and then faster. It ran across roads and fields, submerging all in its path. The Lortons knew that their farm must be flooded, but they had no idea how deep the water had gotten. One of their neighbors, Ed Haz, went to see the flooded area. When he returned, Jeff Lorton asked him, "How high on my second story?" Haz replied, "It's almost up to the window."[8]

Later that day Jeff Lorton climbed into a boat to go see

*W*orkers in Hannibal, Missouri, collect unused sandbags to send to other towns in need. Sandbags were used to strengthen levees weakened by rising river waters.

for himself what was left of the house. He tied the boat up to a second-story window and crawled inside. The water was thigh-deep upstairs, covering everything except the top of the pool table and the high shelves. Lorton gathered together some photo albums and yearbooks that were still dry and put them in the boat. Then he left his flooded home behind. A sign at the entrance read, "Lorton Family Farm. Welcome to Paradise."[9]

The Sny Levee was one of the last to break. When it did, waters from the Mississippi flooded the Illinois side of the river, forcing helicopters to evacuate hundreds of people.

CHAPTER 4

Race Against Time

Quincy, Illinois, is located high on a bluff that overlooks the Mississippi River. Normally, people who live in the town proper have little to fear from floodwaters. Their neighbors, who farm the rich land near the river, also felt safe behind the Sny Levee. The fifty-four-mile-long earth-and-sand barrier was the largest levee in Illinois. It rose seventeen feet above the surface of the Mississippi River. That had always been more than enough height to protect the pig farms and soybean fields along the levee's length—until the summer of 1993.

Worried farmers climbed to the top of the Sny Levee and watched the river water rise higher and higher. Decisions had to be made quickly when the water got to within one foot of the levee's top. Herds of pigs were loaded onto trucks and taken to other farms that were out of the path of the floodwaters. Families quickly gathered up pets, photo albums, favorite toys, clothing, and medicine and went to higher ground.

John Guenseth, who owned a farm close to the river, said that a one-mile stretch of the levee was especially worrisome. The rest of the levee had been rebuilt, but that one-mile part was going to be a problem. Boards would have to be added to the top to make the Sny taller along the weak section. Volunteers faced a huge task as they began sawing and hammering the boards into place. With the water rising an inch an hour, they had to work fast.

Quincy radio station WGEM put out a call for more volunteers. In addition to building the wooden extension, sandbags had to be filled and placed behind the boards to strengthen them. The work was exhausting! There was no shade, and the temperatures soared into the midnineties. When night came, the temperatures dropped a little, but huge swarms of mosquitoes came to torment the workers. Bright lights were turned on, and the volunteers continued to work all night until the two-board barrier was finished.

During this time, radio station WGEM had gone on an around-the-clock broadcasting schedule. The station kept the people who lived in the Quincy area informed about the weather, evacuation notices, and flood predictions. In addition, the station opened its phone lines to callers in the community who needed help or had news to share. An elderly woman called in one afternoon to say that she could not get her belongings to higher ground by herself. Soon afterward, another woman called in to say she was on her way to help.

Several high school girls called WGEM and volunteered to baby-sit for people who wanted to help sandbag.

And when the station broadcast that the National Guard members working on the levee needed dry socks, a local store sent three hundred pairs. WGEM announcer, Bob Turek, said, "The greatest part of this story is the cooperative effort of these people."[1]

As the water rose higher, a third board was added to the top of the levee. Inmates from an area jail were brought over to help with the effort. The prisoners were welcomed with open arms by the exhausted volunteers. As they went to work, the inmates sang and chanted while they heaved hundreds of sandbags into place. A woman called the radio station, complaining that the Red Cross refused to accept her homemade brownies because they only took packaged food. WGEM operator Leo Hemming said, "Ma'am, I'd just take those brownies and stand down by the levee, and I bet you won't have any trouble getting rid of them."[2]

As a fourth board was being added to the top of the levee, a storm began pelting the workers with rain. While water streamed into their eyes and soaked their clothes, a radio message arrived from upstream. Area farmer Kenneth Crim said, "We've got a severe storm warning, with fifty-five-mile-an-hour winds. You have to get off the levee."[3] People grabbed their tools and ran as lightning began to strike around them. Would the levee hold up under the rising river's punishing assault?

The levee held in spite of the force of the thirty-two-foot crest of the river! Kenneth Crim said, "Evidently, we've done something right, wouldn't you say? We're one of the few [levees] still standing."[4] Most of the other levees in the area had failed when the Mississippi River crested, or rose to its highest point. Normally about a mile across, the Mississippi had swelled to nine miles wide in some areas. Writer James Stewart, flying upriver from St. Louis, said, "Small streams were swollen to the usual size of the Mississippi, and in places the Mississippi itself sprawled all the way to the horizon."[5]

On Saturday, July 25, rain started to fall again. Finally, pressure from the rising water was too much for the Sny Levee, and it gave way. An ocean of water poured through a gap in the dirt and sand, eventually covering forty-four thousand acres of farmland with fifteen feet of water. The scene was a grim one. Only the tops of houses and barns were left sticking out of the brown water where once there had been well-ordered homes and green fields.

As the Mississippi River continued its relentless rampage south, St. Louis, Missouri, braced for the flood. Few were worried about the city itself because it was protected by a massive, fifty-two-foot-high levee. Tourists stood by the famous Gateway Arch in downtown St. Louis and gawked at the swiftly moving current in the Mississippi River. Several people from other parts of the country called the Convention and Tourist Bureau to see whether the Gateway Arch was underwater. Frank Vivertio said, "If a six hundred and twenty-foot-tall structure were underwater, we'd be close to the end of the world."[6] St. Louis escaped the fury of the river, but not by

*F*loodwaters rise close to the shore near the famous Gateway Arch in St. Louis, Missouri.

much. On August 1, the Mississippi crested at 49.48 feet, just a little over two feet lower than the fifty-two-foot levee that protected the city.

Fifty-five miles south of St. Louis, the historic town of Ste. Genevieve, Missouri, was a hive of activity. Founded by French pioneers in the 1730s, the town has some of the oldest French colonial buildings in the United States. There were no levees protecting Ste. Genevieve, so volunteers got busy. They started building sandbag levees to try and save the historic district.

As the river continued to rise, a local radio station called for more help. "We have an urgent request. It's raining, and that can create a problem with the levee if we don't keep up. We need sandbaggers and people with pickup trucks to haul bags."[7] Flashlight beams pierced the darkness as residents and volunteers streamed in to help. All night long they filled bags with sand and heaved them on top of the levee to build it higher.

When morning came, children joined the effort, scooping sand into bags with their hands. The schoolyard where they normally played was filled with huge piles of sand. The schools and businesses were all closed, as the people of Ste. Genevieve fought to save their town. More than a half million sandbags were piled onto the levee by the time the Mississippi River crested. Fortunately for the people of Ste. Genevieve, the levee held, and the town's historic district was saved!

CHAPTER 5

Aftermath

On August 9, the crest of the Mississippi River was approaching Cairo, Illinois. At this point in its journey south, the river is wider and deeper than it is upstream; thus it is able to move much more water safely. Once the river had crested at Cairo, the danger of more flooding downstream had passed.

In the rest of the Midwest, the torrential rains had finally stopped. Swollen streams and rivers were gradually shrinking. Falling water levels all along the Mississippi River finally allowed barge traffic to resume on August 24. Coast Guard petty officer Frank Dunn reported, "We're still trying to discourage recreational traffic, but commercial traffic is slowly but surely getting on with business as usual."[1]

When the water began to recede, flooded towns and fields started to drain. Where once there was an ocean of slimy brown water, now there was a sea of slimy brown mud. Inside some houses the mud was a foot deep.

Some people simply refused to let the flood stop their fun.
Joe Gates and Jim Clarkson of Grafton, Illinois, continue
their daily game of one-on-one.

Rotten carpet and moldy furniture greeted thousands of people as they waded into their ruined homes and businesses. Violet Merrigan, postmaster of Pattonsburg, Missouri, described conditions in her town after the flood: "There's the diarrhea and the nausea and the mold, which kind of makes you lightheaded. . . . There's the stench of hundreds of dead night crawlers, and other dead animals all over the sidewalks."[2]

Those who wanted to try to repair their homes and businesses arrived wearing rubber boots and gloves. They were armed with shovels, buckets, and gallons of disinfectant. The work was slow and discouraging, but many were able to reclaim their property gradually. Others just gave up the fight and moved to higher ground. Jeff Lorton and his family did not even try to repair their flooded house in East Hardin, Illinois.

Instead, the Lortons bought fifteen acres on top of Rocky Hill to build a new house. Standing on the hill, Jeff Lorton pointed down to his old house, which was still underwater. "That's my old place way over there. We'll keep the hogs down there, and we'll work down there, but we'll live up here. . . . The house'll be exactly like our old one, except I'll move the living room so we'll have a better view."[3]

Out of 1,576 levees in the Mississippi River basin, nearly 70 percent had failed. More than eighty thousand homes had been damaged or destroyed. Eight million acres of farmland had been flooded, and another 12 million acres were too wet to plant. Fifty-one people died

*M*any businesses lost money because of the floods. Rebecca's in Alton, Illinois, held a "flood sale" to get rid of some of their merchandise.

during the Midwest floods of 1993. The floods also caused an estimated $12 billion in property damages. Congress approved $6.2 billion in flood relief aid. The federal money would help, but it would not be nearly enough to restore lives as they had been before the disaster.

The best part of the summer floods of 1993 was the way people pitched in to help. In addition to local residents, volunteers poured into the area from all over the country. David Moore had lost his house in Homestead, Florida, when Hurricane Andrew hit Florida in 1992. He and his wife, along with seventeen neighbors, loaded their cars and vans in Florida with supplies. They drove all the way to Des Moines, Iowa, to help the town that had helped Homestead in the aftermath of Hurricane Andrew.

In Grafton, Illinois, disaster coordinator Paul Arnold said, "We've had trucks coming in from Dallas and Raleigh, North Carolina, and from Indianapolis, bringing in food and clothing. And here in town, you see people who haven't talked to each other for years out there helping each other move furniture. It seems like when something terrible like this flood happens, all those petty things are put aside."[4] Maybe Pam Christian said it best as she was filling sandbags in the hot sun in Des Moines, "It smelled so bad I was choking. But helping out felt great."[5]

*T*he Midwest floods of 1993 damaged nearly 20 million acres of farmland, including part of Mike McClure's soybean crop in Adel, Iowa.

DATE	PLACE	TYPE OF DISASTER	DEATHS
May 31, 1889	Johnstown, PA	South Fork Dam breaks	2,209
September 8, 1900	Galveston, TX	Hurricane winds and tidal wave	+6,000
June 14, 1903	Hippner, OR	Flooding	325
March 26, 1913	Ohio and Indiana	Flooding on the Ohio River	467
June 3, 1921	Pueblo, CO	Arkansas River overflows	200
March 12, 1928	Santa Paula, CA	Collapse of St. Francis Dam	450
January 22, 1937	Ohio and Mississippi	Flooding of Ohio and Mississippi river valleys	250
January 18–26, 1969	Southern California	Floods and mudslides	100
August 17, 1969	Mississippi Coast	Hurricane Camille pushes wall of water ashore	256
February 26, 1972	Man, WV	Heavy rains cause dam collapse	118
June 9, 1972	Rapid City, SD	Collapse of two dams	263
July 31, 1976	Colorado	Flood on Big Thompson River	139
December 1996	West Coast	Severe floods in California, Oregon, Washington, Idaho, Nevada, and Montana	36

bank—The rising ground bordering a river or lake.

current—The part of a river or stream moving continuously in a certain direction.

dike—An artificial bank constructed to control or confine water.

flash flood—A large flood lasting a short time, the result of heavy rainfall in the immediate area.

levee—An embankment for preventing flooding.

runoff—Rainwater and snowmelt that reach streams.

silt—Fine particles of sand, clay, dirt, and other material carried by flowing water that eventually settle to the bottom.

tributary—A stream or river that feeds into a larger stream or river.

Chapter 1. Triumph and Tragedy

1. Lori Dodge Rose, "Man Swims for It After Rescue a No-Show," *Houston Chronicle*, August 7, 1993, p. A 6.

2. Ibid.

3. "Animals Struggle Against Flood," *Animals*, September/October 1993, p. 4.

4. Dan Guillory, *When the Waters Recede*, Urbana, Ill.: Stormline Press, 1996, p. 71.

5. Ibid.

6. "A Kid's Guide to the Floods," *Houston Chronicle*, July 30, 1993, p. A 3.

7. George Esper, "Cave Flood Survivor Felt He Was Safe," *Houston Chronicle*, July 26, 1993, p. A 2.

8. Ibid.

9. Ibid.

Chapter 2. Weather Patterns

1. Staci Kramer, "Showing No Mercy," *Time*, August 2, 1993, p. 34.

2. J. N. Lott, "The Summer of 1993," *NOAA National Data Center*, <http://www4.ncdc.noaa.gov/ol/papers/summer93/weather.pdf> (January 1,1998).

Chapter 3. Relentless Water

1. Mary Challender, "Water, Water Everywhere . . .," *Gannett News Service*, <http://www.elibrary.com> (May 24, 1996).

2. Bill Bryson, "Riding Out the Worst of Times," *National Geographic*, January 1994, p. 85.

3. "A Kid's Guide to the Floods," *Houston Chronicle*, July 30, 1993, p. A 3.

4. Bryson, p. 83.

5. Pam Lambert, "Trial By Deluge," *People*, July 26, 1993, p. 39.

6. Ibid.

7. Alan Marison, "The Great Flood of '93," *National Geographic*, January 1994, p. 59.

8. Ibid., p. 61.

9. Ibid., p. 51.

Chapter 4. Race Against Time

1. Pam Lambert, "Trial By Deluge," *People*, July 7, 1993, p. 38.

2. James Stewart, "Battle on the Sny," *New Yorker*, August 9, 1993, p. 36.

3. Ibid., p. 37.

4. Ibid., p. 40.

5. Ibid., p. 31.

6. John McCormick, "Troubled Waters," *Newsweek*, July 26, 1993, p. 25.

7. Alan Marison, "The Great Flood of '93," *National Geographic*, January 1994, p. 72.

Chapter 5. Aftermath

1. "Upper Mississippi Reopens to Barge Traffic," *Houston Chronicle*, August 24, 1993, Business Section, p. 3.

2. Robert Famighetti, ed., *The World Almanac 1994*, Mahwah, N.J.: Funk & Wagnalls, 1994.

3. Alan Marison, "The Great Flood of '93," *National Geographic*, January 1994, p. 80.

4. "Ol' Man River," *People*, December 27, 1993, p. 82.

5. Marison, p. 51.

Armbruster, Ann. *Floods.* New York: Franklin Watts, 1996.

Ayer, Eleanor. *Our Great Rivers and Waterways.* Brookfield, Conn.: Millbrook Press, 1994.

Kerrod, Robin. *The Weather.* New York: Marshall Cavendish, 1994.

Knapp, Brian. *Flood.* Austin, Tex.: Steck-Vaughn Library, 1990.

Lauber, Patricia. *Wrestling with the Mississippi.* Washington, D.C.: National Geographic Society, 1996.

Marison, Alan. "The Great Flood of '93." *National Geographic*, January, 1994.

Micallef, Mary. *Floods and Droughts.* Parsippany, N.J.: Good Apple, 1985.

Wright, Russell. ed. Katarina Stenstedt. *Flood!* Reading: Mass.: Addison Wesley Longman, Incorporated, 1995.

Internet Sites

Disaster Information Network: Flood URLs
<http://www.disaster.net/disaster/flood.htm>

Drainage Map of the Mississippi River and its Tributaries
<http://www.greatriver.com/tribs.htm>

Federal Emergency Management Agency
<http://www.fema.gov>

National Oceanic & Atmospheric Administration
<http://www.noaa.gov>

NOVA Online: Flood!
<http://www.pbs.org/wgbh/nova/flood>